This Book Is Given To:

_____

From:

_____

Mischief Meg & Bonnie

Trouble in the Park

By Jane Hiles

In a little town, on the high street,
lives a real Border Collie named Mischief Meg.
Meg is young and silly dog who loves to have fun!

She has an older, wiser sister named Bonnie.
Meg and Bonnie belong to the author Jane,
and this is one of their many adventures...

Every day, Bonnie decides on a job for Meg to do,
she teaches her how to be good and see it through.
So when Mischief Meg, wants to have fun,
Mischief Meg, needs to get her jobs done.

Meg does want to learn, and she is so very very clever,
but her brain then starts thinking faster than ever.
Because of this, Meg gets very very bored,
so she does silly things that can't be ignored.

Bonnie decides the job for today,
is to help at the park and clear the rubbish away.
At the park they meet the warden, go to the bin,
put on their yellow vests,
and put the rubbish in.

Bonnie collects bottles,
plastic bags and cartons,
which Mischief Meg does not seem
to want to take part in.
With her Collie skills, she rounds up the ducks and birds,
and as fast as she can, corrals the squirrels into herds.

Bonnie's bin soon overflows with rubbish stacked neat,
and for her good work she's given a treat.
Then suddenly Bonnie hears a commotion somewhere,
a squeak, quack, tweet from the pond over there!

Meg has a wheelie bin, that's filled to the brim,
with birds, squirrels, and ducks nearby looking grim.
Then Mischief Meg, proud of rubbish she did bring,
began barking a song that she likes to sing:
"Pinky ponky, pinky ponky, run run run,
pinky ponky, pinky ponky, let's all have fun!"

Bonnie runs over as fast as she can,
down to the pond with a wham, zam, bam!
Meg doesn't notice and while being silly and loud,
Bonnie wasn't happy and was also not proud.

Then Bonnie barked loud, like the siren of a cop,
which made Mischief Meg instantly stop.
Bonnie was upset with her sister and it really did show,
making Meg crouch to the ground very nervous and low.

Bonnie shouted, "This is not what we are supposed to do!
We were given and job and must see it through.
We are supposed to be collecting the rubbish and rubble.
If the warden sees this we will both be in trouble."

Feeling bad about her behavior, Meg got up in a flash,
and went back to helping Bonnie pick up the trash.
They set straight to work cleaning up the park,
and started up a happy, sing-songy bark:
"Pinky ponky, pinky ponky, run run run,
pinky ponky, pinky ponky, let's all have fun!"

The ducks are back to swimming,
And the birds are back to singing.
The squirrels are back in their dens,
And the park is peaceful once again.

Bonnie helps Meg collect more for the bin,
and very soon they are all full to the brim.
Now that the park is all nice and neat,
the warden rewards the dogs with a treat.

Mischief Meg has learned a lot today,
that in order to go out and play...
You must first get all your work done,
before you can go out and have some fun!

Now there's only one thing left to do,
since these Collies have seen the job through:
"Pinky ponky, pinky ponky, run run run,
pinky ponky, pinky ponky, let's all have fun!"

♥ Claim Your FREE Gift!

Visit 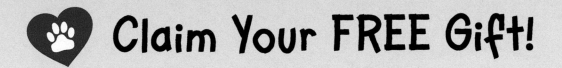 PDICBooks.com/Gift

Thank you for purchasing Mischief Meg,
and welcome to the Puppy Dogs & Ice Cream family.

We're certain you're going to love the little gift
we've prepared for you at the website above.